ANIMAL STRIKE
AT THE ZOO
IT'S TRUE!

BY **KARMA WILSON**

ILLUSTRATED BY

MARGARET SPENGLER

SCHOLASTIC INC.
New York Toronto London Auckland Sydney
Mexico City New Delhi Hong Kong Buenos Aires

ISBN-13: 978-0-545-00007-9
ISBN-10: 0-545-00007-6

Text copyright © 2006 by Karma Wilson. Illustrations copyright © 2006 by Margaret Spengler. All rights reserved. Published by Scholastic Inc., 557 Broadway, New York, NY 10012, by arrangement with HarperCollins Children's Books, a division of HarperCollins Publishers. SCHOLASTIC and associated logos are trademarks and/or registered trademarks of Scholastic Inc.

12 11 10 9 8 7   8 9 10 11 12/0

Printed in the U.S.A.   40

First Scholastic printing, April 2007

Typography by Carla Weise

To Regina, Alan, Chandra, Sabrina, Tyler, and Caleb—
life in your house is as busy as a zoo!
Thank heavens Mommy and Daddy never go on strike.
God bless you all.
—K.W.

To Ken,
my best friend and biggest supporter.
—M.S.

There's an animal strike at the zoo. It's true!

The headlines are telling it all.

The animals quit. "That's it!" "We're through!"

Say all critters from biggest to small.

We're Through!

"We're paid only peanuts!" the elephants shout.

"And goodness, we're bigger than that."

So now they won't trumpet or lumber about.

They sit in the shade, looking fat.

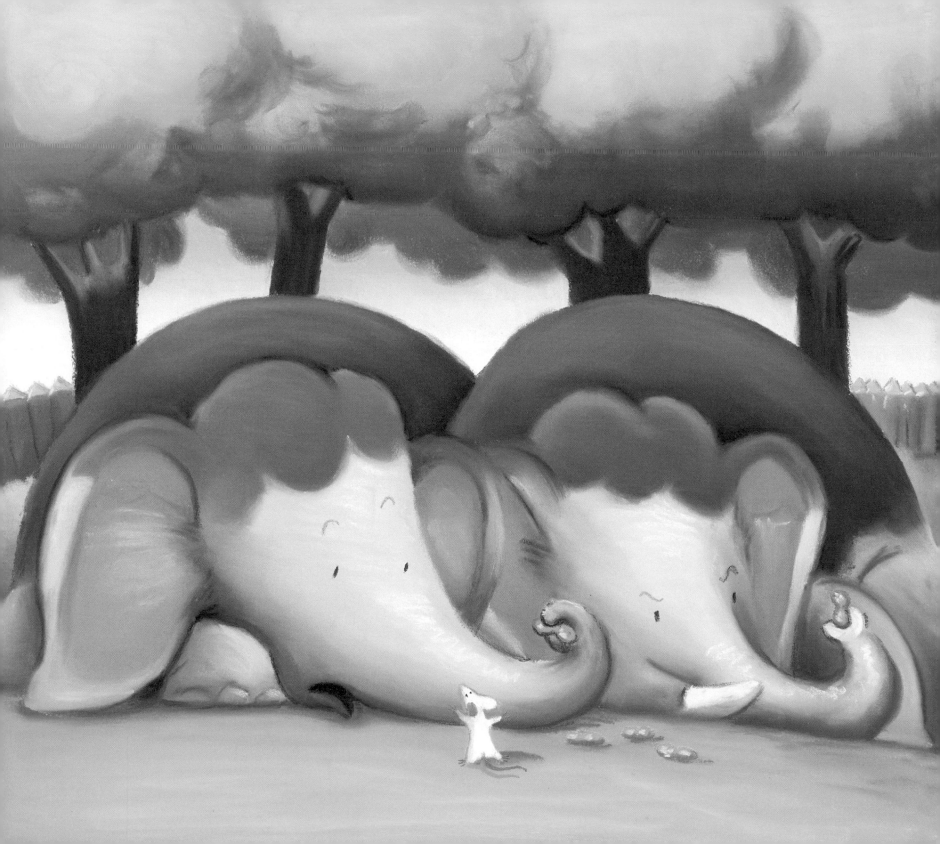

The monkeys won't monkey around anymore.
"You won't see us climbing again!"

They wallow like big monkey lumps on the floor.

"We want a nice pool in our pen!"

The leopards aren't prowling.

The wolf packs aren't howling.

The tigers aren't growling.

The otters are scowling.

EGAD! The worst has come true.
There's an animal strike at the zoo!

The zebras are looking like horses today.

They painted their stripes in, you see.

"We're all sick and tired of eating this hay!

Our good looks do NOT come for free!"

Those silly giraffes are not any better.

"You won't see our necks anymore!"

They're knitting themselves lots of turtleneck sweaters,

Which go from their heads to the floor!

Business these days is as slow as can be.

Folks go to the circus instead.

Nobody wants to pay money to see

The animals lying in bed!

The lions aren't roaring.

The eagles aren't soaring.

The penguins are snoring.

It's all rather boring.

What can the zookeeper do?

There's an animal strike at the zoo!

He really is doing the best that he can.
The elephants all got a raise.

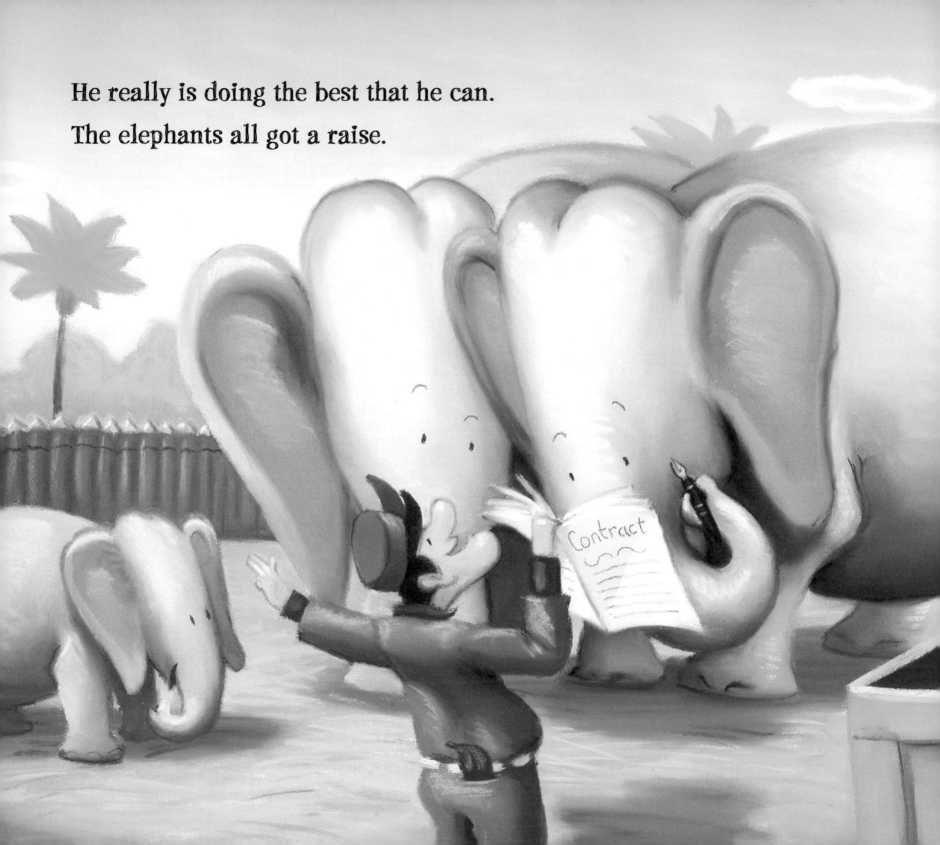

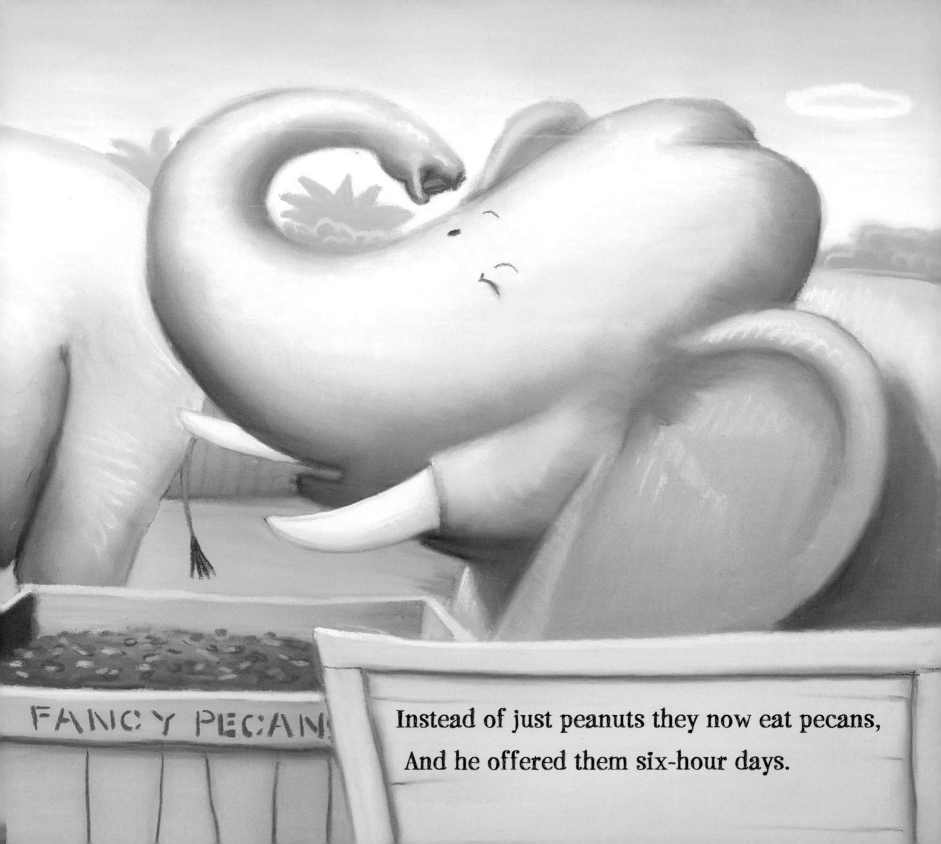

FANCY PECANS

Instead of just peanuts they now eat pecans,
And he offered them six-hour days.

The monkeys were given a small kiddy pool,
And he's feeding the zebras sweet oats.

But the monkeys complain that the water is cool,
And the zebras demand root-beer floats!

Then in through the gate walks sweet little Sue.
She just can't believe that she's here!
She's always wanted to come to the zoo,
And she's begged for this trip for a year.

But . . .

No birdies are peeping.

No lizards are creeping.

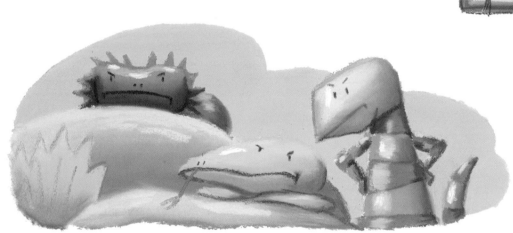

No bunnies are leaping.

Then poor Sue starts weeping.
Her heart is broken in two . . .
By the animal strike at the zoo!

As tears start to streak down her cute, rosy face,

The animals watch that wee child.

A deep hush of sadness falls over the place . . .

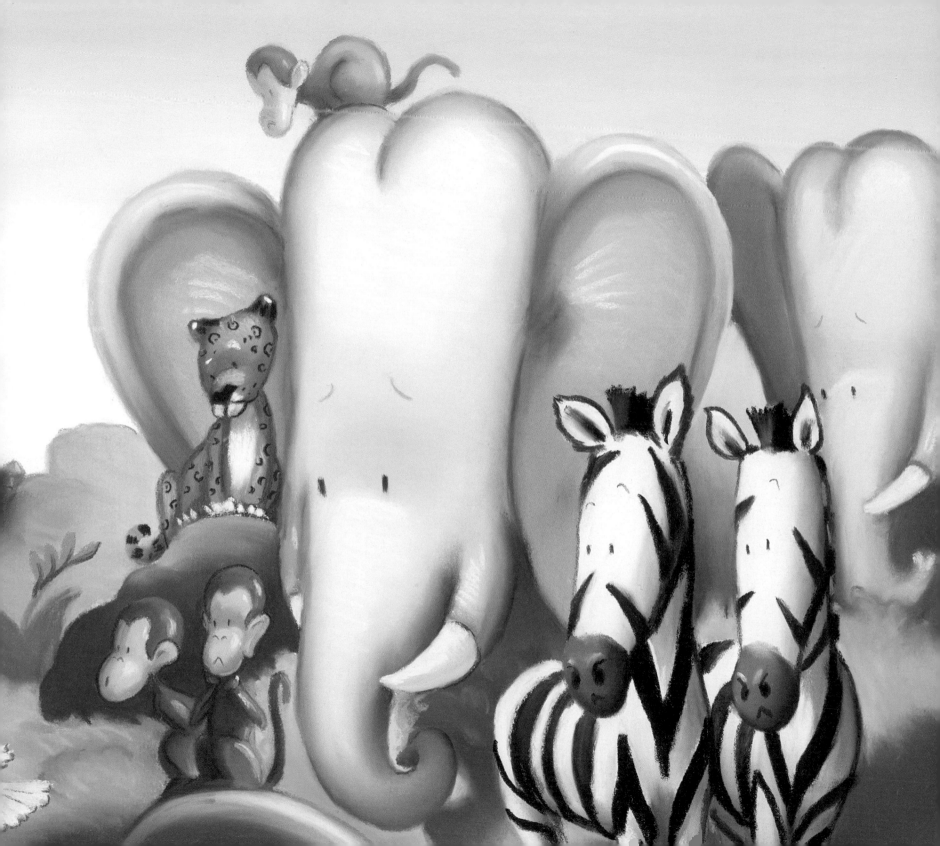

And then they go

TOTALLY WILD!

With roaring and peeping and howling and growling,
All critters from biggest to small
Start soaring and creeping and leaping and prowling. . .

Then little Sue laughs at them all!

And all of the animals find out that day
They actually like what they do.
The zookeeper calls the reporters to say,

"HURRAY! NO MORE STRIKE AT THE ZOO!"

But . . .

The bear at the circus won't pedal his bike.

Uh-oh. He says he's on strike.